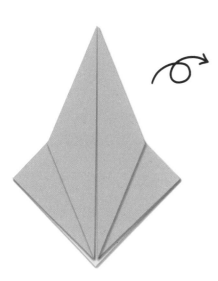

9. Flatten boat shape inward.

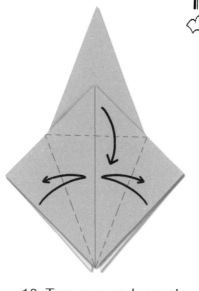

10. Turn over and repeat folds on the other side.

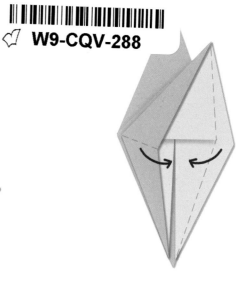

11. Open to boat shape then flatten.

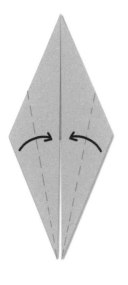

12. Fold sides of top layer to middle.

13. Does it looks like this? Then turn over and repeat the folds in step 12.

14. Reverse fold the bottom points.

15. Reverse fold one point.

Your finished crane!

Origami
PEACE
CRANES

FRIENDSHIPS TAKE FLIGHT

Sue DiCicco

TUTTLE Publishing

Tokyo | Rutland, Vermont | Singapore

Emma's family had just moved to town, so Emma had to go to a new school. She was so nervous! She wanted to look just perfect. She tried on about a million-billion-trillion outfits. "Without a special outfit I'm just me," thought Emma. "And *me* is not enough!"

Too plain.

Too flashy.

Too hot.

Too hoody.

Too tutu.

Too much.

Too little.

Too late!

It's getting late! Emma will be late! Pick something, Emma!

Emma looked through her magazines. What hairstyle was right for her? "If I don't have a special hairstyle I'm just me," thought Emma. "And *me* is not enough!"

Too plain.

Too flashy.

Too much.

It's getting late! Emma will be late! Pick something, Emma!

When Emma arrived at her new school, she didn't see anyone dressed like her, or wearing their hair in an up-do. "Oh no! What if no one likes me?" Emma thought. "Why of all those million-billion-trillion outfits did I pick this one?"

Inside the classroom Emma saw a cubby with her name on it. As she put away her lunch, a boy came over and put a lunchbox in the next cubby. It was a super cool lunchbox, just like the one Emma saw on TV.

"Hi! My name is Kumar!" said the boy.

"Whoa!" thought Emma. "That lunchbox is so amazing. And his hair is so curly and cute. He seems really awesome. But I'm just me. And *me* is not enough. Kumar will never want a friend like me." No. Nope. No way.

Emma found a desk with her name on it and sat down. A little paper crane was on her desk. Emma saw there was a different colored crane on every desk and every crane had a special message written on its wings.

As Emma looked around, a girl sat down at the desk next to her.
"Hello," said Emma.
"Hola!" Juana replied.
"Hola?" thought Emma. "She can speak another language?
That's so cool. But how will I ever talk to her if I don't understand
what she says? I don't know another language. I'm just me. And
me is not enough." Emma knew Juana would not want a friend
like her. No. Nope. No way.

At lunchtime Takako sat down next to Emma. She opened a box with many compartments that were full of rice and fish, and little, colorful pickles. Emma looked at her own lunch. It was a peanut butter and jelly sandwich. "My lunch is so plain and boring. Why would anyone with an amazing lunch like that even want to sit next to me?" thought Emma. No. Nope. No way. Emma thought Takako would never want to be friends with her.

On the playground, Emma saw Elizabeth and Rafael playing together.

"Hi, Emma! Do you want to play?" called Elizabeth.

That sounded like fun to Emma! But then she saw that they were playing a game she had never played before.

"I don't know how to play that game," thought Emma. "I wouldn't know what to do." No. Nope. No way. Emma thought Elizabeth and Rafael would not want to be friends with her.

At recess Emma sat alone. Suddenly, she saw that the bow was missing from her dress. And her up-do wasn't so up anymore. It had all fallen down. No bow, no special up-do. "Now no one will want to be friends with me," Emma thought.

"I'd like to play with Emma," Kumar told his friends, "but she doesn't want to be friends with me."
"Me too!" said Juana.
"Me three!" said Takako.

After lunch Emma found a new paper crane on her desk. "Some people call these *peace cranes* and use them to send messages of peace and friendship," said Emma's teacher. "Let's fold peace cranes and write messages to each other on their wings!"

Soon everyone was working carefully to fold the colorful cranes. They wrote messages on the wings, then placed them on the desks of the other kids. "No one will ever want to trade cranes with me," thought Emma. "I'm just me. And *me* is not enough." No. Nope. No way. Emma was not making friends. But she would try.

When Emma returned to her desk she was surprised to see it covered in peace cranes. She picked up each crane and read the messages on the wings. All those messages were written just for her!

The crane from Kumar was super cool! He had painted feathers on the wings. The message he wrote asked Emma to be his friend. Emma liked art and thought Kumar's crane was really great.

And maybe Kumar really did want to be friends! Maybe he didn't care if Emma's hair wasn't just right, or her dress wasn't special. "I'm me!" thought Emma. "And maybe *me is* enough!"

Juana made a really colorful crane. In her message she invited Emma to come over and play with her dog. Emma loved dogs! "Would I need to learn some Spanish to visit Juana's house? Maybe Juana could teach me," Emma thought. "I can learn something new. Because I'm me! I can do that! And maybe, just maybe, *me is* enough!"

Takako's peace crane was covered in drawings of ice cream cones. Ice cream cones were Takako's favorite thing in the world, and they made her happy. Emma liked ice cream too! "Maybe Takako and I can have ice cream together some time," thought Emma. "That would be so cool! I can try the flavors she likes, and she can try the ones I like. Maybe being me is okay sometimes!"

Elizabeth and Rafael both gave Emma peace cranes covered in soccer balls. "Wow, they like soccer?" thought Emma. "I like soccer too!" Who needed a bow and a special hair style? Emma could play soccer in her favorite shirt and sneakers. Elizabeth and Rafael wouldn't even care. "Wow!" thought Emma. "I can just be me. Because *me* is exactly who I should be!"

Before she knew it, Emma had many new friends, each special and unique. Sometimes she tried new things with them and learned about new foods, games and ideas. Sometimes she liked those new things. And sometimes she didn't. "But," thought Emma, "as long as I'm *me* I'm exactly who I should be!"

When Emma's schoolmates came over to play Emma forgot all about their differences. They were all exactly who they should be. Sometimes they were a little goofy. Just like Emma. Yes. Yep. Yessiree. They were all perfect, just as they were. And each of them became a good friend to Emma.

One morning Emma saw a new family moving in across the street. They looked very different from Emma's family. Would they ever be friends?

Emma knew just how to welcome her new neighbors! She showed her mom and little brother what she had learned at school. They all carefully folded cranes for the new neighbors and wrote welcoming greetings on their wings.

Emma put on her favorite dress and wore her hair exactly how she liked it. She was looking forward to making new friends. "I'll just be me," thought Emma. "Because *me* is who I should be. *Me* is exactly perfect!" Emma placed the folded cranes on the new neighbors' doorstep.

The next day, Emma and her family all met the new neighbors. They were fun and they liked hanging out with Emma's family. The kids showed Emma some cool new games. The dad brought some new kinds of food they had never tasted before. And Emma's family got to share things they liked too.

As the weeks went by, Emma folded cranes for everyone she met. Now everyone in town knows Emma and always gives her a big smile and wave. No matter their differences, where they are from or what language they speak, Emma calls them all "friend" because she is perfect, just as she is. And so are they. Yes. Yep. Yessiree.

Published by Tuttle Publishing, an imprint of Periplus Editions (HK) Ltd.

www.tuttlepublishing.com

Library of Congress Control Number: 2017940671

ISBN 978-4-8053-1466-1

DISTRIBUTED BY
North America, Latin America & Europe
Tuttle Publishing
364 Innovation Drive
North Clarendon, VT 05759-9436 U.S.A.
Tel: 1 (802) 773-8930
Fax: 1 (802) 773-6993
info@tuttlepublishing.com
www.tuttlepublishing.com

Japan
Tuttle Publishing
Yaekari Building, 3rd Floor
5-4-12 Osaki
Shinagawa-ku
Tokyo 141 0032
Tel: (81) 3 5437-0171
Fax: (81) 3 5437-0755
tuttle-sales@gol.com

Asia Pacific
Berkeley Books Pte. Ltd.
61 Tai Seng Avenue #02-12
Singapore 534167
Tel: (65) 6280-1330
Fax: (65) 6280-6290
inquiries@periplus.com.sg
www.periplus.com

First edition
20 19 18 17   6 5 4 3 2 1

Printed in China   1706CM

ABOUT TUTTLE:
"Books to Span the East and West"

Our core mission at Tuttle Publishing is to create books which bring people together one page at a time. Tuttle was founded in 1832 in the small New England town of Rutland, Vermont (USA). Our fundamental values remain as strong today as they were then— to publish best-in-class books informing the English-speaking world about the countries and peoples of Asia. The world has become a smaller place today and Asia's economic, cultural and political influence has expanded, yet the need for meaningful dialogue and information about this diverse region has never been greater. Since 1948, Tuttle has been a leader in publishing books on the cultures, arts, cuisines, languages and literatures of Asia. Our authors and photographers have won numerous awards and Tuttle has published thousands of books on subjects ranging from martial arts to paper crafts. We welcome you to explore the wealth of information available on Asia at **www.tuttlepublishing.com**.

the PEACE CRANE project

I founded the Peace Crane Project in 2013 as a way to educate children through the arts, promote peace and understanding, and connect students around the world.

We are an international exchange program, inviting families, schools, community groups and individuals to fold an origami crane, dove, heart or another symbol of peace, write a message of peace on their creation, then trade it with another group on our exchange list. We publish our list of exchange partners and aid in connecting our members, year round.

The Peace Crane Project gives children the opportunity to express themselves creatively. It offers them a chance to connect with other students around the world. They learn basic geography, strengthen their writing skills, improve their hand-eye coordination, are exposed to other cultures, given the opportunity to hear new languages, and see the world through the eyes of others.

Visit https://PeaceCraneProject.org to sign up!

You will receive our newsletter, which includes instructions and suggestions, each week. Many groups join us as part of the United Nations International Day of Peace celebration in September. But we host the Peace Crane Project continuously and have members looking to connect every day of the year. Please participate anytime that works for you.

Questions? We are here to help. Please contact me.

Sue DiCicco
sue@peacecraneproject.org

Photo by Jen Thym

How to Fold an Origami Peace Crane

Blue represents the front side of the paper. Yellow represents the back. Your paper may look different.
To participate in The Peace Crane Project you will need a square piece of paper,
plus markers, pens, paint, or pencils.
For help in folding your crane see the video on peacecraneproject.org.

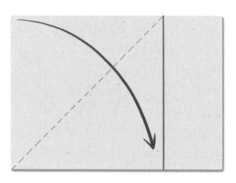

1. Fold your paper in half, diagonally.
If your paper is not square, cut along the red line.

2. Fold in half again.

3. Bring top point of top layer
down to meet bottom point,
opening paper as you go,
to form a square.

4. Does your paper look
like this? If so, turn it over.
If not, go back to step 3.

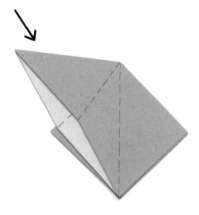

5. Repeat fold on this side.

6. Fold sides of top layer
to middle, then unfold.

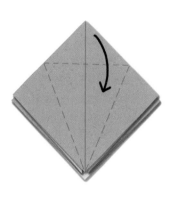

7. Fold top down to side creases,
then lift top layer upward.

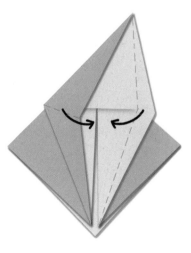

8. Create a boat-like shape
by folding sides inward.